Caren L. Bock
Judy C. LaLanne
11·17·05
Susan Felli

CREATED BY HOSPICECARE OF SOUTHEAST FLORIDA, INC.

Acknowledgments

This book is written for parents and children who are
coping with a loss. It is often difficult for a child to
express their feelings when they lose someone, and for
parents to know how to encourage sharing. We hope
this story enables you to communicate your inner most
thoughts with each other.

To my wonderful parents, thank you for sharing all of your
talents and time. I love and cherish you!

To my loving husband, John, thank you for your inspiration
and support.

To our children, Brittany, Ashley, Brooke and John II,
thank you for every minute of happiness and love you have
given us since the first day we held you in our arms.
I love being your mother!

With Love,

Caren J. Bock

Caren J. Bock

© 2005 HospiceCare of Southeast Florida, Inc.

Photos by Stark Photography, Inc.
starkpht@bellsouth.net

Text © 2004 by Caren J. Bock
Illustrations © 2004 by Judy C. Schwinghammer
Edited by Terry A. Dargan and Caren J. Bock

For information regarding permission to reprint material from this book, fax request to HospiceCare of Southeast Florida, Inc. at 954-467-3353; or email your request to cbock4@aol.com; or mail your request to HospiceCare of Southeast Florida, Inc., 309 S. E. 18th Street, Ft. Lauderdale, FL 33316; or visit www.hospicecareflorida.org.

Published by Wyatt-MacKenzie Publishing, Inc.
15115 Highway 36, Deadwood, Oregon 97430
www.WyMacPublishing.com
Specializing in Empowering Mom Writers

Library of Congress Control Number: 2005926538

Publisher's Cataloging-in-Publication

Bock, Caren J.
    Wings a story of transformation / written by Caren J. Bock :
Illustrated by Judy C. Schwinghammer – First Edition.   p. cm.
    SUMMARY: HospiceCare story of a caterpillar's transformation and
a boy who learns to deal with change.
    Audience: Juvenile
    LCCN: 2005926538
    ISBN: 1-932279-12-1

    1. Dealing with death–Juvenile Fiction. 2. Change and transformation–Juvenile
    Fiction. I. Schwinghammer, Judy C., ill., II. Title.

Printed in China

Dedication

To Christopher, Angelo, Ann Marie, Penny, Adam, Paul and Papa Telly for teaching us that death is another way to share your life.

To Lisa May and her family for allowing us to share in their experience.

To Hospice Hundred for inspiring us and creating a connection between all involved through education, membership and fundraising.

To our dear friend and colleague Pat Byrnes, who is our rainmaker and makes us shine.

To our friends and family, who continue to give us courage to help others.

And to all our loved ones who now have their **Wings** – You are missed but never forgotten.

~ Susan G. Telli & Caren J. Bock

Susan G. Telli reading **Wings.**

Introduction

Adults have a difficult time explaining death to a child. We are fearful we might frighten or hurt them. After all, children shouldn't have to deal with something as "sad" as death. But what do we say when a beloved pet dies? How do we help a child to understand when Grandma is very sick and may not live much longer? What does a child think when we tell them that Daddy has "gone away?" What is "gone away?"

Wings is an understandable analogy between the life cycle of a caterpillar and our own life and death. We move from one phase to another and we are transformed into our own special "butterfly." Children are very literal, what we tell them and the words we use, becomes their understanding of reality. Children learn in school how caterpillars become butterflies. A cute, fuzzy little insect becomes a colorful, light as air, butterfly – a change of form, gone from our sight but never forgotten.

We hope that **Wings** will make it easier for adults to explain how all of us, regardless of age, make the transition from life to death.

Wings

a story of transformation

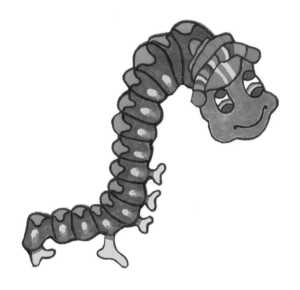

written by Caren J. Bock

illustrations by Judy C. Schwinghammer

inspired by Susan G. Telli

Wyatt-MacKenzie Publishing, Inc.

DEADWOOD, OREGON

Today was a special day, it was the first day of summer.

Christopher was excited because he had an important meeting at the sandbox. Every afternoon he would be able to have playtime with his best friend.

He quickly ran over to the window which overlooked the sandbox to see if his friend was waiting for him. After grabbing one of his toys, he ran out of the room, down the stairs, and out the back door. He stopped only to tell his mother he was going to the backyard.

As Christopher ran outside there was Fuzzy, his best friend, sitting on his baseball next to the sandbox. Fuzzy was a long and colorful caterpillar that always wore a big smile.

"I wasn't sure if you were coming today," said Fuzzy.

"Have I ever missed before?" asked Christopher.

Fuzzy looked up and said, "Not that I can remember, you always seem to make it."

"What did you bring to play with today?" asked Fuzzy.

"I brought my model airplane, because I know how much you like to pretend to fly," said Christopher.

Fuzzy turned with his big smile and said, "Thanks."

The two played all afternoon until his mother called from the kitchen window, "Christopher it's dinner time."

"See you tomorrow Fuzzy," Christopher said.

"Bye," said Fuzzy.

Christopher hurried to the house.

The next day, Christopher ran over to the window. He looked around the yard and couldn't *see* Fuzzy anywhere. They would play hide and *seek*, but Fuzzy never played without telling him.

Christopher went out the back door and stopped by the garden to *see* if Fuzzy was eating one of his Mom's prized tomatoes. He wasn't in the garden.

Then he went to the sandbox to see if Fuzzy was in the castle they had built the day before. Fuzzy wasn't there. Christopher went over to the huge oak tree in the corner of the yard to *see* if Fuzzy was climbing like they both did *so* many times before. He wasn't there either.

Now Christopher was very worried. Fuzzy was nowhere to be found.

There was only one place left that he could *be* and that was the swing. Christopher and Fuzzy always had fun on the swing. He would *sit* on Christopher's shoulder as they went higher and higher. Fuzzy always *said* he was born to fly.

As Christopher walked to the swing, he saw Fuzzy sitting on the tire. But he didn't have his smile.

Christopher thought something must be very wrong.

Fuzzy looked at him with his big purple eyes and said in a soft voice, "My sister, Annie, entered her cocoon today."

"What is a cocoon?" asked Christopher looking puzzled.

"A cocoon is a nest where caterpillars enclose themselves before they change into butterflies," Fuzzy said.

Christopher still puzzled asked, "Why do caterpillars turn into butterflies?"

"My mother told me that in our life we go through different stages. First, there is the life of the caterpillar which is made up of long days of eating and resting to build a healthy body. As we grow our spirit grows with us. As time passes our spirit becomes too big for our caterpillar body so we slowly change into a butterfly," Fuzzy explained.

"So your sister is going to be a butterfly? They are *so* beautiful with all the colors they have!" Christopher said with excitement.

"Yes, they are *beautiful*, but one day they must fly to the peaceful garden where all butterflies go," said Fuzzy.

"Why do they go to the garden?" asked Christopher.

"Butterflies need to have quiet spaces with *beautiful* flowers and waterfalls," replied Fuzzy.

"Why would your sister leave you?" gasped Christopher.

"She isn't really leaving me," said Fuzzy. "Annie is going ahead to wait for me. She knows that I have time left to be a caterpillar and that I will *be* with her when it is my time to change. I am really going to miss her."

A couple weeks later, Christopher was in his room playing with his model airplane when he noticed a large butterfly outside his window. He couldn't take his eyes off of it. Then suddenly the butterfly flew into the air spreading its wings. Christopher wondered if that was Fuzzy's sister.

Rushing out of his bedroom, and out the backdoor, he ran past the sandbox to the big oak tree that Fuzzy loved to climb. There was Fuzzy on one of the top branches watching the butterfly in the sky.

"She is beautiful," exclaimed Christopher.

"I know. I know," said Fuzzy. "That is my sister, Annie, and I am going to miss her very much. She sure is colorful isn't she?"

"Yes, she is," said Christopher.

Fuzzy and Christopher continued to play together. He loved to bring his model airplane so Fuzzy could pretend to fly.

Fuzzy would cry out, "Someday I will be flying too."

This upset Christopher. He went to Fuzzy and asked, "Are you going to leave me?"

"Yes Christopher, one day I will enter my cocoon, and then I will fly away," Fuzzy said.

"I will miss you Fuzzy," said Christopher.

"I will miss you too, but just remember, every day I will be in a place that makes me very happy. I will also be with my family who is waiting there for me," said Fuzzy.

Christopher looked down at the ground and quietly said, "I know... I know..."

As the summer went on, Christopher kept seeing Fuzzy change. Day by day his friend started to look different. Christopher noticed his friend was playing less, moving slower, and sleeping more. As the summer grew to its end, Fuzzy told Christopher that he wanted a very special day with his very best friend. They thought that the last day of summer before school started would be perfect. It was only one week away.

The last week the two played every afternoon. They would swing as high as they could, climb the old oak tree, make sand castles, and would even go into his Mom's garden so Fuzzy could take a bite of her delicious tomatoes. The summer was perfect, but it was time to tell Christopher what was about to happen.

Christopher was excited about seeing Fuzzy since it was their special day. He rushed out of his room and down the stairs. He stopped to see if his mother would give him a tomato to celebrate the last day of the summer with his best friend.

"Of course," said his mother.

"Thanks," said Christopher.

He took it from his mother's hand and ran to the back-yard where Fuzzy was waiting in his red fire engine.

"Christopher you are early today," Fuzzy said.

"It is our special day together and I didn't want to miss anything," Christopher exclaimed.

"It is our last day, and I am going to miss you," Fuzzy replied softly.

"But we will still have the weekends together Fuzzy," Christopher said.

"It is time for me to start making my cocoon. My spirit has grown too big for my body and it is time for me to start my next journey," said Fuzzy.

Christopher was very quiet as they walked to their favorite swing.

"If you leave who will be my *best friend?"* questioned Christopher.

"I will always *be* your best friend. I will *be* waiting for you in a special place," Fuzzy said. "So for one last time let's swing and *see* how high we can go."

Christopher hugged Fuzzy as they swung very, very high. Fuzzy was right by Christopher's shoulder. They both imagined they had Wings.

The next afternoon when Christopher came home from school he couldn't find Fuzzy anywhere. He looked in the garden, in the sandbox, by the huge oak tree, and even around the swing.

Each day for the next couple of weeks, he continued to look for him. Christopher could not stop thinking about his friend.

One morning, outside of Christopher's window he noticed the most beautiful butterfly he had ever seen. Christopher stared as the butterfly flew off the branch and landed onto his window. This butterfly wore a big smile.

Then it took off high, high up in the sky, fluttering in the wind, and showing off its' beautiful colored Wings.

Christopher was excited because this butterfly smiled just like Fuzzy. He knew this was his best friend. He ran as fast as he could down the stairs, and out the back door.

As tears rolled down his cheeks, Christopher shouted and waved, "Bye Fuzzy, I am going to miss you!" Fuzzy flew back towards Christopher, gave one last big smile, waved his wings and soared high into the sky.

Christopher was sad to see his friend fly away, but happy because Fuzzy always wanted his Wings.

"If nothing ever changed, there'd be no butterflies."

~ Unknown

About the Illustrator

Judy C. Schwinghammer received her BFA (Cum Laude) from Indiana University where several of her art pieces received purchase awards and remain in the permanent art collection. She gained considerable experience in children's art as an art instructor for Holy Family Elementary School, New Albany, Indiana.

The inspiration for this artwork relates to challenges she experienced as a young child with a disability. She received treatment for polio at Gillette Children's Hospital and Camp Courage in Minnesota where she developed friendships and experienced loss at an early age. Through these illustrations she hopes to reach out and help others.

The illustrations in this story were rendered in pen and pencil using Prismacolor. The images and the technique are the original creation of the artist.

Judy wishes to thank her husband, Dan, and daughters, Caren (author) and Kristen (legal counsel), for their love and support throughout this project.